THE NIGHT I LOST MY FATHER'S GUN

The Testimony of Elon X

Azmi Abusam

Dedication

For my beautiful mom and dad. Thank you for making so many sacrifices and teaching me how to live.

For my brother and sister. Thank you for enabling this book. You mean the world to me.

For my family and friends. It's a pleasure to experience life with you amazing humans. I love you.

BOOK 1

CHAPTER I

Double Murder

What I'm about to tell you may sound far from the truth, but I swear on my mother's life that this is what happened the night I saw murder with my own two eyes. To make a long story short, my father had gone away...once again. Principal Morrison wanted me gone, and Mama suggested some sort of military school in God-knows-where Montana, but I needed to stay in Southeast. I would've been extremely depressed and lonely out there in the Rocky Mountains. Probably suicidal, if I'm being honest. Something about the lonely mountains could drive anyone to the point of insanity.

But things weren't going well last December.

Aside from art I was failing almost every class, and more importantly, things were getting crazy between my girlfriend and I, Zanie Hurston, and her best friend Sade Walker. These two girls had me Googling the concept of multiple soul mates and diving deep into rabbit holes about love. Although, to be honest, after my sleepless nights Googling the secrets of how to tell if someone loves you, I always came back with more questions than answers, so I gave up knowing who loved me the most.

To give you some context, Zanie used to say extremely cheesy things like, "our love was strong enough to hold together a hundred marriages", and this was probably true. Sade, on the other hand, was astonishingly beautiful and more mysterious than Zanie could ever be, which I think attracted me to her. My buddy used to say, "nine out of ten women in D.C. would murder their own mothers to look half as good as Sade."

These girls were no strangers to receiving attention anywhere they went, but when it came to this, where Zanie was far more well-rounded, Sade was more conceited. Sade also had this sixth sense of knowing when me and Zanie were going through turbulence. After fighting one day, Sade invited me over to look at one of her paintings, and because I was mad at Zanie and part of me wanted to make her jealous, I went.

Her painting wasn't finished, but from what she had shown me, I could tell it was going to be amazing. That afternoon, she said she had a birthday present for me, but that she wouldn't give it to me unless I found her Friday night at the party. When I told her that I wasn't sure I'd be able to make it, she didn't believe me. I would have stayed longer and tried to convince her, but her father was on his way back home and he was the type to murder you on sight, whether you had been engaged in disgraceful behavior or not.

I was lost in thought on my way home that day, part of me still mad at Zanie, our fight replaying in my head over and over, and the other part wondering what was going on with Sade. Sade and I had met through Instagram, but technically Zanie was the one who introduced me to her outside of the internet. I met her on the first day that I'd been transferred to Frederick Douglass, a charter school in Southeast, which was probably six or seven miles away from the White House. The waiting list had about three thousand people, but my father had business with the chancellor which undoubtedly came in handy with my enrollment.

Mama said Douglass was full of "gang banging hustlers and fast girls," but I was more focused on graduating and playing college ball than any of those stereotypes. But that Friday night changed everything and my father, if he's reading this, is probably saying "real men stay ten steps ahead"... and he knows better than anybody that you can't always see it coming, so I should probably learn to take his advice more seriously.

CHAPTER II

Snooping Into My DM's

T he Friday afternoon before winter break had officially started, two gummy bear eating security guards escorted me to my locker without putting any respect on my name. I let it slide because I was already in too deep and the school had cops posted up outside next to paddy wagons. I cleaned out my locker, said goodbye to a couple teachers, and ran into a couple friends at the cell phone check-out line.

"Yo, Ava, Veronika, what up ladies?" I said. "Y'all coming out tonight or what?"

"Boy, you know me and Ava ain't missing it. Obviously it won't be poppin' until we walk in," said

8

Veronika. She was wearing all black, as usual, with a hoodie that said, "When Melanin Is The Plug."

"Well, I know you're gonna' be there, probably twerking upside down, but aren't you still grounded?" I looked Ava up and down. My mom would've killed my sister if she had been dressed like that.

Ava rolled her eyes dramatically. "Boy, please! I'm on technology punishment—I'm not missing out on those Jell-O shots."

"They better figure out a way to keep 'em cold, cause last year it got way too hot and stuffy—and by the way, Elon, I like your beard, but go like that, there's crumbs in there," Veronika said, reaching out and scratching her fingers on my chin.

Ava busted out laughing. "Veronika, O my God! This boy got Doritos in his beard!"

"Not all of us could be blessed with a great beard like you, Ava," I smirked, fluffing my beard.

"You ain't nothing but a hater, boy," Ava said. "I know I'm popping. But Vee, remember, you walked into that party with those natural curls and came out with a messy bush, I told you to use my flat-iron —"

She was copying Cardi B's voice. As I tuned her out, I started imagining holding a fistful of Sade's hair like the night we kissed at her spot. I didn't know much about women's hair, of course, but Sade used to tell me the frizz came from humidity, or something like that, and she obviously knew how to take care of hers from the looks of it.

"...the flat iron wouldn't have made a difference, but either way, I still walked in there looking like Tracy Ellis," said Veronika.

"By the way, girl, Felecia was doing my hair last week and she was telling me the Italians be drinking wine at breakfast and they found some little islands where people been living past a hundred and fifty with all this luxurious hair," said Ava.

"Hmm," said Veronika. "Well, it sounds like these people found the elixir of life."

Ava went off, "So they did an investigation and found out most of them had been on a Mediterranean diet, drinking coffee, adding olive oil to everything and sitting around talking junk—"

I jumped in, "So, basically, the community keeps you living at the end of the day, you know, and all this technology is making us smarter but more depressed."

Her message didn't fall on deaf ears. I enjoyed what she had to say, really. I had gotten into biomedicine after seeing that scientists had extended the life of a worm by one hundred days. They discovered aging could be reversed, and some scientists had been saying super old people would be playing contact sports competitively pretty soon. I was skeptical about a few things because the science was still young. I mean, only God could imagine how much knowledge we would never be able to possess, and I kept working out and eating clean just to be safe, but I knew between genetic engineering and virtual reality, the world was on a revolutionary wave and I wanted to be on the right side of history.

"Yeah, speaking of community," Ava continued, "Sophisticated Ignorance has never been about getting dolled up and staring at that digital leash. It's about dancing and having fun, escaping back into reality and experiencing real life."

I smiled, "You're blessed to be on phone punishment."

She chuckled, then leaned in towards Veronika and I and said in a low voice, "The location is still to be announced or whatever, but my cousin said it's supposed to be at a huge mansion in Maryland with a heated pool and everything."

"You need a gold bracelet to get into the water," Veronika said. "It's not for everybody."

"Somebody told me they rented the place online and did a deal with a private security company," said Ava.

I didn't even know that was legal, but I guessed that meant it wouldn't get raided this year. I knew I'd have to Google the laws around the private security thing because it could've been fake news.

Next to me, Ava flipped her hair over her shoulder, and I noticed for the first time the new tattoo on her forearm, still shiny with the lotion you're supposed to put on as they heal.

"Whoa!" I said. "What's this? You got a new one?"

"Yup, it's my fourth one," Ava told me. "I got it last week, but for some reason, it's taking forever to heal."

"Commuter bona profundere deum est," said Veronika.

"To pour benefits for the common good is divine," Ava responded.

"I told her to get it in Arabic like Rihanna," said Veronika, then she turned all of her attention on me. "But what's up with you and Zanie? Are y'all still together or what? Spill the tea, boy!"

"Yeah, we're still talking or whatever," I said, then narrowed my eyes at her. "Why? Did y'all hear something?"

Honestly, I always got paranoid, wondering if these girls had a plug in the NSA; reading my Googles, snooping into my DMs, seeing all my thoughts. Sade would never talk, right? At least, that's what I had hoped.

"I mean, there's some people claiming you're single, and some girls saying there's something going on between you and Sade," said Veronika.

Ava cocked an eyebrow at me knowingly. "You know we see the way she looks at you when Zanie ain't around."

CHAPTER III

Dog Filter Selfies (3:30 PM)

Veronika kept bugging me for information about my status with Zanie. I offered her zero details and changed the topic back to the house party. Some of Veronika's friends were kind of close with Zanie, and those girls were always gossiping and talking junk.

After waiting in line for a few minutes, I got my phone back out and there were a ton of notifications. I had so many texts from people asking me about getting expelled and the group chat was chaos. A bunch of people were online talking about Sophisticated Ignorance getting busted the year before.

They say the cops pulled up, blocked all the

exits, and wrote everybody up for underage drinking. Some people got hit with charges for possession and others got locked up that night for carrying...I was supposed to be there that night. Thankfully, the team was out of town for the playoffs, which had turned out to be a blessing in disguise.

"Did y'all hear anything else about the special performance at SI," I asked, steering the subject back to safe ground.

Veronika nodded. "Somebody said Meek, Shy Glizzy and Oddisee all live in that same gated community."

"Manzanita, I think that's the name of the neighborhood."

I whistled. "That's close to Ellicott City. That area is supposed to be nice."

"The special performance must be a rumor somebody started to get people hyping up the party," Ava said.

"Lil' Wayne said he doesn't even go to the club unless they're paying him. Dude values his time—y'all gotta see some of his interviews. They're good," Veronika said.

"Yeah," Ava said. "I love those old documentaries. It seemed like all he wanted to do was stay in the studio and make music and skateboard."

"If I got on a skateboard, sis, I would break every bone in my body. I don't know how my future baby daddy could get into that," Veronika laughed.

"He said it took his mind off of everything," I said. "If you're thinking about anything else, then that's how you end up in the hospital."

"Shoot, all of us might end up in the ER after SI," Ava giggled.

"Watch, somebody's gonna overdose or have to get their stomach pumped, and there's always some fights with some random wannabe thugs from Maryland," Veronika said.

"I wanna know who's giving them the address!" Ava made a disgusted noise and glared around like she could find the culprit in the students still milling around us.

"I don't know, but maybe it has to do with everybody going live and tagging the location," said Veronika.

"SI has that Everyday People vibe, so I think everybody feels welcome," I said.

"But these folks ain't showing up to have fun," said Veronika. "They're coming for a different reason."

"Like what?" I asked.

"You know this boy always wants an example,"

Ava snorted.

"Well, my cousin's best friend from Baltimore told her Magic City likes to buy guns in Maryland and flip them in D.C.," said Veronika.

"Sounds like Yuri in *Lord of War*," said Ava.

"Yup, precisely—and now these scammers pushing that money into Canadian bonds and Chinese startups."

"Sounds sketchy, sis," Ava said.

"When I make it, I'm only going to my own house parties and every plus one will have to be approved in advance."

"It has to be like that—these days, everybody ain't for you and you ain't for everybody," Veronika said.

"Mhmm, life's already unpredictable as it is, and people change up all of the sudden, real dramatically, so you really have no choice but to keep your circle small," said Ava.

But even with all that drama, everybody knew Sophisticated Ignorance was one of the best parties in the D.M.V. It had its own identity, rules, and traditions.

I said bye to Veronika and went back upstairs to get a few things out of my locker, and my phone was still blinking. Somebody posted a picture of a house that looked like one of those secluded palaces in Spain. It looked old, with a 19th century vibe and lush gardens all around the perimeter. The undisclosed location for the party, no doubt.

On my way out of the building, I said goodbye to a few cool teachers, custodians, and lunch ladies. When I walked outside, everybody was kicking it in the parking lot, blasting the new Travis Scott album, and some guys from the team were posted up on the fence eating hot chips.

One of my cousins was with them rocking the new black Yeezys, drinking grape soda, and his ratchet girlfriend was hanging on his arm, taking dog filter selfies and chewing bubble gum with her mouth open.

I switched my phone to vibrate and walked across the lot towards the baseball field where my squad assembled. Grayson Brennan and Amir Tayeb were already there, chilling on their phones. I wasn't sure if we'd see our boy Pablo Guzman since he cracked his skull open popping wheelies on a dirt bike by the Harris Teeter in Noma.

Right at that moment, I got a text from Zanie, and my phone buzzed in my hand. *You better not go to that party tonight!* it read. *You promised to take me to the movies. If you go...it's over.*

She was acting crazy and being melodramatic. I rolled my eyes and shut off the phone without bothering to respond. My father always said "don't spend your youth chasing women", and I never forgot that. A couple minutes later, Sade sent me a DM with some emojis. I went to her page and saw her new selfie, which already had more than five hundred likes in a couple hours. She knew she was bad. She just wanted to remind me.

I greeted the guys and sat down, pulling out my phone again and scrolling through Instagram without seeing the pictures that went past.

Zanie was complicated.

We were together...but not together. All I knew was that we had a good flirt to roast ratio. She loved to talk junk about my anger problems and me seeing a therapist, and I'd constantly make fun of her for being a clingy hood booger, but when it came to being exclusive, I knew nothing about that. To be honest, I avoided that conversation like swine.

My relationship with Sade was so different.

With Zanie, we'd usually kick it on the weekends and do random stuff like go shopping in Georgetown or hit up Rock Creek Park where nobody would recognize us. Zanie exposed me to all this weird nature stuff like hiking at Sugarloaf and

Billy Goat. The last time we were out there, I stole a flower from each garden and made her a dope crown. I got to know her pretty well. She had this idea of us settling down on a huge farm where we could swim two miles a day in the ocean, go hiking, sleep in caves, paint for ten hours a day, eat from gardens of blueberries, plant mango trees, milk cows, slaughter our own sheep, and raise fat goats.

On the hikes, we would spot deer and run into foxes that didn't seem to be afraid of us. Sometimes she would tell me I wasn't ready to see certain things because I had become "so alienated from nature" and "the world was full of unverified animals, living just beyond the edge of human knowledge."

One time last Spring, after watching YouTube videos about building a fire, we made smores and spent half the night looking at the stars and the moon. Times like that she would have deep conversations with me about love, family, challenges, the seasons of life, and all the other random things clouding our minds.

She was brilliant like that. You could tell Zanie had been paying attention in class, doing all the reading or whatever, but when it got dark, she got very close to me because "she was afraid of bears." I told her all those books couldn't protect her and that black bears were less threatening than the brown ones. I wasn't even sure if that was true, but that's what somebody had told me after they'd spent the summer with family in Alaska.

Sometimes after spending the day with Zanie, Sade would invite me over for dinner. I'd usually bring dessert and flowers and make her laugh, but part of me felt guilty about being with the two of them on the same day. But if you could taste Sade's cooking, you'd understand why I fell in love with her. She was all about experimenting in the kitchen, copying fancy dishes from high-class food magazines and world famous chefs. Sade wasn't intimidated by complex recipes and directions.

One time she made this amazing fish for me using wild roses, hazelnuts, smoked paprika, kosher salt, lemon, and she soaked it in pickled seaweed and some other herbs, I can't remember exactly what kind, and blueberries as well. To her, cooking was both an art and a science.

But Zanie must have sensed her competition—especially after going through my phone when I left it unlocked. I'm sure she wanted to be the one putting gourmet on my breath, so I wasn't surprised when she started cooking for me too.

Last Valentine's Day, Zanie had gone all out and

made this roasted lamb that I still get cravings for. We ate that on the couch and watched *Anamnesis*, one of her favorite shows about salvation in the next world and remembering stuff from your previous life. The weird stuff that she was into. I wasn't sure if I was supposed to be with Zanie or Sade, but I knew my addictive personality dovetailed almost perfectly with everything about them.

CHAPTER IV

Finesse

As soon as I started thinking about the painting Sade would give me, Amir showed up rocking a sick coat and matching One's. He stayed fresh, mostly because his cousin had a startup in Silicon Valley, but his parents cut off his allowance in November when they caught him selling his ADHD medicine.

Pablo and Grayson popped up a couple minutes after Amir, and since it was Friday, everybody was showing out, wearing their best outfits. Grayson with his Helly Hanson as red as blood, and Pablo was wearing some rare retro J's as usual. We met up after school every Friday and rapped about sports, girls, music, and anything else that could snag our interest. The four of us went way back, and our kinship was more than constant companionship. We had a real camaraderie, and everybody kept it one hundred.

Sometimes Grayson would smoke, and the guys would rag on him about it until he walked away. Amir had asthma and Pablo was on probation, and he wasn't into it anyway, ever since he did some time in juvie and got exposed to Buddhism or something. Now he was more into cleansing his body and staying healthy, which was good for him, to be honest, because he had been living between foster homes, with occasional nights in his girlfriend's attic.

His biological mom almost had citizenship status, but ICE came for her because she had been hosting immigrants, mostly single mothers, lost children, and old people with dimentia. Unfortunately, so many countries were being ripped apart inside-out. But that's probably why Pablo's empathy was solid. Besides, I wasn't interested in his mom's vices.

The point was, everybody knew about my clique and they were familiar with our reputation. We didn't tolerate disrespect from anybody and it was pretty obvious we were the most popular dudes at

Frederick Doug. We didn't take academics too seriously, but most of the time, by the grace of God and with a lot of help from our girlfriends, we still made the honor roll.

We rode dirt bikes around the city, we could shoot straight with any gun you put in our hands, and we would be the ones holding our liquor like real gentlemen at Sophisticated Ignorance. It wouldn't be like that one night at the beach when I accidentally mixed light and dark and blew up my pants—luckily that story never got out. That's when I knew Pablo was my ride or die goon.

When we got to the top of the hill, we got to talking about the DJ playing new music until we heard the screams from the brawl.

CHAPTER V

World Star

Me and the guys could see everything from our vantage point because we had been high on the hill. Down below us, surrounded by a growing crowd, Sophia Nix grabbed the other chick by the locks and threw her down against the fire hydrant, landing two jabs and a nasty uppercut. Chloe Emerson the student body president, rose up pretty fast, kicked the other girl in the mouth and got blood all over her cheetah print Nike's. Some people were hollering, and I couldn't tell whose side they were on.

The violence was obviously over the new quarterback. Rumors had been swirling around the locker room for weeks. Nobody was surprised. If anything, we wondered why it took so long to go public. Mama always said, "a jealous person was dangerous because they were possessed by a mad devil and a dull spirit."

The fight only lasted for a few minutes until Assistant Principal Hughes stormed out the cafeteria with three security guards to break it up. Nobody liked him because he tried too hard, and nobody took the security team seriously. They couldn't scare you more than a jealous woman. The crowd of kids around the fight jeered and laughed at the security guards as the men tried to break the girls up.

You might think it's weird that girls would fight so ferociously, but that's just how things were around my neighborhood; a punch to the face was the most direct type of communication, something that couldn't be misinterpreted. Just last week, a dude got sent to the ER with a broken nose, swallowed teeth, and a ruptured spleen. It seemed like people with too much pride couldn't control their ego, and usually, they were the first ones to learn about the thin line between life and death.

Most people around here tried to earn respect by having a predatory attitude or by having the "right look"—blowing their money on name brand clothes—but at the end of the day, everybody knew what was happening in our neighborhood was because our community had lost some of its faith in the judicial system. That's probably why my father used to say, "a petty fight about nothing wasn't worth being locked up."

My father was an OG, so I always listened carefully when he spoke to me about the game. Even though he had an impressive collection of pistols and ARs fitted with scopes as if he was El Chapo, he wasn't attracted to violence. He was all for the Second Amendment and common-sense gun laws and he simply wanted to protect his family. Before he went away, I remember him warning me about revenge being the cousin of ignorance. He thought it was the best time to be alive even though technology had been "robbing us of our days."

When the police finally showed up, everybody tried to act like nothing had happened, and the crowd dispersed. Sophia and Chloe had already been dragged, still screaming at each other, inside. The cops talked to a few people who stayed, and we walked down the hill past them. From what I heard between a few of the cop's radios, there was a something going down by the Pink Store, the corner store up the street. Pablo said it was Magic City, the same dudes who felt some kind of way when I turned down their offer to join their gang.

Amir laughed. "Bruh, is it just me, or did it look like those girls were using some moves from Mortal Combat? And how did security not know this was going down today? Everybody's been talkin' bout this rematch forever."

"Yeah," Pablo said. "The girl with the dreads...I can't remember her name, but she's a savage. I know her and Dimitri got caught under the bleachers last year before a game and they almost got suspended."

"See, to me, that sounds like favoritism," Grayson chimed in. "But Mia told me there's supposed to be a rematch tonight, especially since the party's gonna be crazy."

Amir grinned. "It's definitely about to go down tonight for sure. And ain't that the same girl who told you she had a boyfriend at the skating rink, but she was single?"

"Bruh, that whole clique thought they were so bad, but if they went to New York or Atlanta, they might get a reality check."

Amir smiled wryly and looked at Pablo out of the corner of his eyes. "But who are you when beauty fades?"

"Save that garbage for your lame podcast and those two followers you have," Grayson said, smacking him on the back of the head.

Amir just shrugged. He had a way with women, and we all knew it. Girls always liked him because he had this philosopher vibe. But I'd known him long enough to realize the truth; he just watched a lot of Oprah's Super Soul Sundays and he had goals of making his own show. He was the type to say something like "genius outlasts beauty" and actually mean it.

I realized I had spaced out for a second, wondering who had the right mix of genius and beauty: Zanie or Sade.

"New York has the most beautiful women in the world, bruh," I said. "But everybody says it's too expensive."

"New York is dope and all, but I'm moving to Atlanta, homie, that's supposed to be the new Hollywood and my cousin said there's so many smart, super fine women down there—all over the place—looking for a good dude."

Amir said, "I think you can find your soulmate in any city, to be honest, but Flannery O'Conner used to say a good man is hard to find."

"Yeah," I agreed. "You just gotta know how to be loyal and treat a woman like a queen."

Amir nodded. "Women don't get enough credit if

you ask me. I mean, if it wasn't for them none of us would be here, brother. They have the divine power to create life and we don't."

We must've been talking for a while because the baseball field lights came on and the dance team walked out of practice. Pablo was watching them eagerly.

"I wonder if Olivia and them are going to be there tonight." Grayson groaned and rolled his eyes.

"She needs to stop giving you those lame excuses —you should already know whether she's going to be there, straight up," Pablo said. "You're man enough to deal with the rejection and keep moving forward."

I didn't really know what they meant by rejection. "Oh, by the way, I forgot to tell y'all, I watched that OJ documentary the other night and it seems like this ninja got away with committing." *That must be why my father said everybody's capable of evil, they just need the right trigger.*

Grayson kept up with my quick change of topic.

"Yeah, but did y'all know about the Kardashian connection? They said Kris Jenner was sitting in the courtroom with her new man while her old man defended her side piece."

"Whoa," Pablo said. "I never heard about that,

but it sounds like Dimitri's situation, right? His girl-friend caught him cheating, but she was still in love with some other dude anyway."

Amir snorted. "She should've ended that rela-tionship instead of giving him a false sense of hope."

Pablo shrugged, his hands in his pockets. "This stuff ain't always clear cut."

"If you ask me...loyalty is pretty clear cut." Amir said, and Grayson and I nodded in agreement.

"Speaking of loyalty, Dimitri was stupid for leav-ing a trail of likes," I began, but before I could finish speaking, Dimitri walked up.

Grayson, playing it smooth like always, quickly said, "Look here, bruh, the situation ain't always black and white, but the party is supposed to be crazy tonight."

He barely missed a beat.

Dimitri jerked his head at us in greeting. "I was just about to ask y'all about the party. What time y'all getting out there?"

Coincidence like this had me very paranoid. I was extremely superstitious, and Dimitri was always giving me bad vibes, anyways. I also used to see him talking to Sean and some dudes from Magic City.

Amir answered for all of us. "Probably around like eleven or midnight."

"If E stops playing around and gets the car to-night," Grayson jabbed.

Dimitri grunted. "I'm stealing grandpa's whip to-night, too, bruh. I would let y'all ride, but I already got four people riding with me."

I must've gotten really distracted because the next thing I remember is them going back to girls.

"Let me tell y'all something," Grayson said, look-ing like he was giving a lecture. "The secret is to keep 'em on read and not respond too soon. My momma used to say, 'you lose a lotta money chas-ing women, but you ain't never lose women chasing money.'"

Amir laughed and slapped him on the back.

"Facts all day, bruh. Momma ain't never lie."

Just then, Zanie double texted me about going to the pop-up movie theater by Union Market. I knew it would be a good show, but that was also her way of keeping me from going out with the guys. I left her on read, once again, for trying to finesse me.

CHAPTER VI

*Three Flames and the
Kissy Emoji*

I n retrospect, I should've known it would be a crazy day. I got sent to the Principal's office first thing Friday morning, and spent most of the afternoon at In School Suspension, with Sean.

Yes, Sean King, the leader of Magic City.

Yes, the same one whose cell phone exploded last summer leaving him deaf in his right ear and blind in his left eye.

Some people said he'd deserved it because it happened a few weeks after he knifed a dude in an alley for being gay. Obviously, I had no business speaking to him. After doing a few hours, security let me go say goodbye to some friends, but under heavy supervision like I was a serial killer.

I had a good reputation around here before the party, and before word got out about my dad's half-brother, Uncle Wayne. A lot of people heard about the FBI accusing my Uncle Wayne for allegedly running a distribution ring in Northern Virginia. I didn't believe it, and Pablo always talked about how often the Feds lock up the wrong guy when it comes to murder.

He said the Feds would fudge the numbers because people would lose their minds if they knew how many serial killers were actually out there, just chilling, uncaptured. One of the detectives who took my Uncle down used one of Sean's people as an informant—that situation didn't ease the tension, especially since Sean had some family working with the cops, and supposedly, it was everything from prosecutors to maximum security guards.

I didn't know too many of Sean's people and King wasn't a common last name in Southeast, but I saw one of his older cousins about a year ago at Ronald Reagan. He pulled up in a black Suburban, opened the trunk, and a woman climbed out with her hands tied behind her back. But that wasn't as bad as Amir's sister being kidnapped during broad daylight. She was special. She was three years older than us and already had a few scholarships lined up and job offers from NASA.

Nobody knew if she was dead or alive, and Amir's family would never get answers. We all knew it and after a few weeks, everybody was already mourning a different murder. Veronika said nobody cares when a black girl disappears, it's not like they ever saw her in the first place. The public investigators pretended like they had leads but then dropped off because they don't get paid enough to care. Meanwhile, Amanda Knox still had some headlines.

Side Note: Sean didn't need that family and Fed drama to have beef with me. He felt some type of way because Sade had been his girlfriend still when she'd asked me to study with her. See, most people were intimidated by Sean; he strangled his neighbor's Pitt last summer for barking too much and punched a cop for being rude to him.

Sade and I sat next to each other in class, but that's just because Mrs. Payton created the seating chart. When I told Sade about the dog, you know she flipped out. She loves animals more than anything, probably more than people. After she blew up at Sean about it, she started hitting up my line more often. Sending me snaps, double texting, triple texting, calling and FaceTiming me even when Zanie was around.

She would give me paper notes in class the old-fashioned way, telling me she wanted to be exclusive and how I was looking like a snack. So of course things escalated fast, the same way they always do with light skinned women, and we did the best we could to keep it on the hush. But once Sade commented three flames and the kissy emoji under one of my photos, Zanie became suspicious.

My page was on private and Sean wasn't following me, of course, but I wondered if somebody would send him a screenshot. There were always wolves disguising themselves as allies, so, naturally, I knew things would pop off, especially if I ran into Sean at Sophisticated Ignorance. Most likely, he would be there. Everybody showed up to SI. Nobody missed the biggest party of the year. However, Sean and his fake friends didn't know me well; I was just like my father. If you threw me to the wolves, I was the type to come back with a fur coat.

CHAPTER VII

The Story That Bleeds

We talked about the fight, the party, and then we got Pablo up to speed on the girl who got murdered in the neon glow of a McDonalds in Northern Virginia. Nobody had all the details and the investigation was still open, but the media was acting like they had answers. Sometimes all that commentary was nothing but speculation.

The press loved clickbait, especially since bias had become so pervasive. Mama said it would be hard to end the new wave of misinformation and ignorance sweeping through so many countries and nobody knew who would handle the responsibility of stopping the unenlightened perspectives.

She used to watch interviews with the parents and tell me I better never make her go dead in the eyes with grief like that. Mama was prone to some crazy wild stuff, so I listened when she spoke like that. She had this solemn ferocity which made grown men second guess themselves. I wish you could see the way she spoke at customer service when she was returning stuff without a receipt for the original value. She was sharp like Johnnie Cochran or Atticus Finch and she never accepted store credit either, only straight cash.

Maybe the medicine made her numb and the drinking certainly got out of control, but you still couldn't sleep on her because she was just as much of an OG as my father. To be honest, I missed seeing them together in the kitchen, especially around Christmas, burning popcorn and making chocolate chip slice 'n' bakes, while arguing about love and politics and religion, and sometimes fights about stuff I wish I'd never heard.

I guess there had to be some truth to people saying ignorance is bliss or whatever. I always thought Mama would've been so much happier if she never found out about my father's two other baby mommas, but I never told her that.

Amir spoke, jerking me back to the conversation

that had been going on around me. "Bruh, from what I heard, this dude was definitely on one and he came back drunk from a party and that's when he ran into the girl and her friends walking down the middle of the street."

There's a bunch of different versions of this story already," Grayson snorted. "Some people say the dudes on the street did nothing wrong, some people say somebody threw a water bottle at him, and I heard some other folks say the driver was talking mad reckless."

Pablo shook his head. "You never know what people are on around two in the morning—you can't take no risk like that, and you never know what they got in the trunk."

"What's sad is how nobody went back to help that girl up when she fell down and dude came back swinging a bat..." Amir trailed off.

"Man, to be honest, those dudes could've done more to help." I growled. "I mean, these dudes should've been ready for this man to pull up and hop out with a loaded gun."

I remembered my father talking about "embracing solitude during chaos" and how that can keep you alive sometimes.

"Bruh," Pablo said. "This dude killed shorty for

no reason and now some other dudes from Virginia wanna protest the vigil even though the Constitution talks about freedom of religion."

Amir scoffed, rolling his eyes. "They talkin' bout it's a hate crime and what not, but in my opinion, homeboy prob'ly thought he'd get away with it... y'all remember when them girls went missing?"

Pablo kicked a rock, scuffing his foot on the ground. "Yeah, those girls got no Amber alert, probably because they're dark and you know I don't even believe in conspiracy theories or play the race card like that."

Grayson pushed him. "Nah, you actually stay believing in some dumb stuff and you click on all the links for fake news—y'all remember what this man said the other day about ball players shutting up and just dribbling—out here reading all the wrong stories."

Amir laughed a little at that. "Well, you know there's a lot of underreported stories, like so many issues that are not getting enough attention."

"Man, you know they're trained to lead with the story that bleeds, and they been doing that since like the nineteenth century or something, or whenever journalism was born," I said.

The guys agreed. "Yeah, it's been bout money and

views and now they got more competition with the internet," Amir said.

"Yeah, well, the internet created a space where everybody wants to be. I mean, now people jump off to escape back to reality...but not for too long," I said. "The internet's weird, y'know? It leaves you alone, but at the same time, it encourages human interaction."

Pablo turned to Amir suddenly. "By the way, all that nonsense y'all were saying in the group chat last night was wrong, dude. Steve Jobs would've come up with the concept for the iPod whether he did those drugs or not. The man was a genius."

I laughed, nodding. "I'm sure Steve had a bunch of dope ideas on deck anyway, way before he did any of that. I mean, this dude knew he had an idea that was gonna revolutionize the world before he even dropped outta college..."

"Everybody remembers Steve Jobs, the genius, and now we got Musk, bruh. But people forget Steve had two dudes on his team doing code and putting ideas on paper. The other dude came with the business mindset, just like Mitch. Steve was like Don Corleone—"

The conversation got heated as usual until somebody finally changed the subject to getting some stuff for Sophisticated Ignorance, then to the Zanie and Sade drama, and eventually we got back to arguing about the murder. Everybody wanted to be the hero, but not enough dudes were built with enough courage to do something when drama goes down. The world was full of posers, cowards, and wolves who felt tough just because they had a gun. But these guys probably couldn't even shoot under pressure. Matter of fact, so many of them would just stay outside and do nothing like that security guard from the Parkland shooting.

CHAPTER VIII

OG Instincts (4:30 PM)

Mama was picking me up that day, so I needed to be sober. Plus, smoking was becoming more and more of a habit, but it was making all of us so stupid, killing so many brain cells. I left the guys just as they were lighting up and walked to the front loop by the library, scrolling through IG. A few foreign model's pictures slid up my screen as I scrolled past.

A few minutes later, after I'd crushed a bag of salt and vinegar chips and watched some people across the street sneak dissing, Mama pulled up in daddy's black Impala. Her car was in the shop and she wouldn't be able to buy a new transmission until her next paycheck. I offered to pay half but accepting dirty money "went against her principles."

She didn't say a single word when I got in, and I could tell from the look on her face that she regretted the day I was born. She had been in rehab for a while because of an addiction and assaulting a man who always let his dog poop on our front yard, but she'd been released a few months ago. We were still getting used to one another again. I rolled down my window and didn't look at her as we pulled away from the curb.

Once we got to the red light at the corner of Minnesota Avenue, I saw a man posted up by the metro escalators selling small bottles of perfume. He was wearing a furry brown trapper and tough looking military boots, with the bottles hanging across his chest like machine gun ammunition.

Just then, Sean King and his crew came up the escalator smoking Newports and playing 21 Savage on a bluetooth speaker. You could tell they were scheming and plotting, and I thought I heard one of them say my name, but that was right before mama pulled off. Whether I'd imagined it or not, I knew that now I'd have to carry protection to Sophisticated Ignorance.

If Mama hadn't picked me up that day, I probably would've taken the metro and ran into those dudes. I preferred taking the metro over riding with Mama's annoying self. It was free with a school ID, but tons of stupid dudes got arrested all the time for jumping the gate. Unfortunately, a lotta dudes around here didn't realize D.C. probably had some of the most undercover agents in America. Pablo called them freelancers in plain clothes who blended in with tatted up sleeves and concealed weapons. He said after a while, with some experience, you'd get better at reading people and understanding who was too vigilant to be an ordinary citizen.

"Right there...that's your future, boy," Mama said, speaking suddenly when we stopped at a light. She pointed to two homeless men who had been digging through a dumpster next to the Popeyes.

"You see them crackheads, don't you? That's exactly where you're gonna end up since you wanna play around in school and not do no work."

She slapped the steering wheel in cadence with her diatribe, her rings and bracelets punctuating her point like usual. This was petty compared to what had happened the last time my Father went away, and I didn't know whether to feel relief or prepare for some unrestrained rage to come out later on—she was the type of woman who had two sides that acted like they ain't even know one another.

The homeless guy with a dirty duvet wrapped around his neck like a cape pulled a biscuit out of the dumpster. The other man was wearing denim overalls with busted up Air Max sneakers and a red Tyrone Biggums-looking beanie. I didn't think they'd be brave enough to light up in broad daylight, but my Father taught me early never to sleep on dudes with nothing to lose.

I had a feeling Mama was about to give me another one of her lectures about education being the vehicle for mobility. Even though she never made it past a few years of college, she was constantly reading everything she could get her hands on and because of her interesting flavor of oral dexterity, she spoke with so much certainty about everything. It was so annoying.

"And I'm tired of talking to you—you're stubborn, and dumb, and you don't listen to nothing... your sister went to the same schools and she never had any of these problems."

"First of all," I snapped back. "She was in the academy and you need to stop comparing us...we're two completely different peo—"

"Shut up, boy, we raised you and Diamond the same way but she ain't lazy like you and she knows how to get stuff done, but you'd rather follow those fake friends of yours instead of doing something productive with your life."

"My friends ain't got nothing to do with this—"

"Let's see how much your friends care about you when you dead, broke, or in jail. And you must be stupid if you think somebody's gonna hire a dumb seventeen-year-old who couldn't graduate from high school. But go ahead screw your whole life up. That's what you want, right?" She practically screamed the last part, and then said, "Park the car."

Without waiting for me to answer, she opened her door and got out, leaving the keys in the ignition and the car in the middle of the street. I knew she was shaken up real bad...she only does dangerous, impulsive things when there's too much stress on her mind and no real outlet.

She stomped into the clinic for her appointment and everybody stared at me like her acting crazy was my fault, so I changed the station to Hot 95.5 and acted just as bewildered as them, just like James Brown. They were playing commercials for a second-hand university and some fake attorneys, and behind me people kept honking, so I figured now was as good a time as any to slide to the driver's side and park.

I wanted to play my own stuff, but my phone died again, the battery was jumping from thirty percent to being dead just like that. To be honest, I had a crazy feeling Apple was controlling the battery. I thought I was crazy for thinking that, but then I remembered my father saying something about real men understanding their instincts and knowing how to make an observation and articulate.

The weather woman came on after the commercials, giving more information about a nasty snow storm heading down from New England. She had an accent like Sophia Vergara, and apparently, D.C. hadn't seen a blizzard like this in over a hundred years, but everybody knew even Hurricane Katrina wouldn't keep folks from going to Sophisticated Ignorance.

I wondered how difficult it would be to drive in the snow, but people said D.C. did a good job cleaning the streets and laying down salt. Anyway, maybe I was feeling just as impulsive as Mama, so even though her lecture kept swirling around in my head, I was committed to going out. I had too much on my mind to be serious and SI would probably be the last time I got toasted with the homies and enjoyed quality minutes with Sade. If I didn't show up, everybody would call me Sean's punk and I wasn't afraid of anyone except for God.

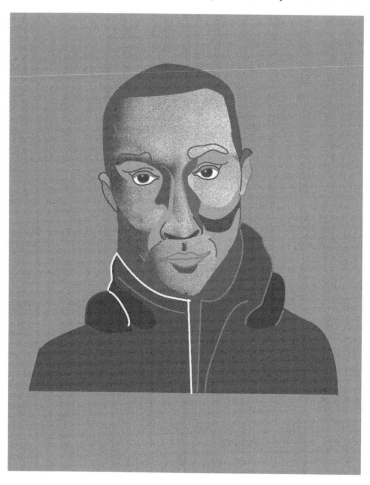

CHAPTER IX

A Vet in Chinatown (5:30 PM)

I swung by the cinema and the only good thing playing was the new *Star Wars*, but I didn't know how to feel about new powers being given to the wrong folks and important characters getting killed off like the Red Wedding. After leaving the theater, I accidentally made eye contact with a homeless man when I turned the corner onto 7th. He was wearing a turtleneck and some Goodwill looking Chelsea boots, holding a cardboard sign that read "Vietnam War Veteran Will Work For Food."

There was a cricket caught in a spider web hanging out right behind him, but he apparently wasn't aware of it. The spider looked poisonous, and I knew that from binge watching all of Planet Earth. Zanie would play it for me some nights when the silence was unbearable. She'd get sweet almond oil and rub my feet, and she'd take it so serious, too, as if by soothing the muscles, eventually she'd get around to the heart, which was really just another muscle after all.

The homeless man's situation reminded me of a conversation I had with my therapist about Maslow's pyramid. Ever since then, whenever I saw human suffering, I wondered what the government was doing about it. My father had opinions about homelessness and world hunger. He saw the world as the enemy until proven innocent and warned me that men get played when they move as if they know everything.

He said, "You gotta lay low with your eyes wide even if you have the sauce." My homeboys used to joke that my Father looked like Fetty Wap. I thought losing his left eye made him see the world different, as if the right eye got sharper than most people's two ever would.

Sometimes I thought I'd trade either of my eyes for my Father's perspective, the way he saw right through people. Call him pessimistic, maybe, but me and Mama knew it kept us all safe. I didn't have all the banter to back up my politics yet and that's why I never contested my Father. He would have beaten me down to size in seconds.

But in the Nation's Capital, wasn't there some space where this man could suffer a little less, at least be afforded the human right to basic privacy? Maybe you'd see something like this in San Francisco and Atlanta, but not here. People came from all over the world to D.C. to capture the essence of America in a selfie.

How could we build monuments to wars and not throw anything toward the people who didn't die from them yet, the ones suffering from PTSD in front of everybody because they had no other choice? I guess that's why some people said "politics was the art of compromise, making things possible, and always finding the next best thing."

"Sir, I wish I had more coins for ya, but this all I got...and I think you should watch out for that brown recluse behind you, they're poisonous." I handed him the change in my pocket.

"Boy, this more money than you think. The nickel in here worth six point eight cents. Imma stack 'em up, stack em up, stack em up. Let these platinum bars double up. The dollar might fall apart. That's why you see everybody jumping on the crypto." He put his hands back in his hoodie's pouch.

"Everybody and their grandma has been mining coins and looking for cheap energy. I know some people who had machines running all day and night until the Feds sent out helicopters with geo thermal detection."

"Look, youngblood, things about to get very crazy. Some of these countries about to go bust. Boom. Boom. Real talk. Everybody out here speculating, not knowing which way the coin might land."

"Probably like you when you got back from Vietnam."

"Vietnam was a nightmare, boy, and not just because we lost millions of good men, but when you kill someone under dubious circumstances, your life will eventually turn into hell."

"So, what happened when you came back? I thought if you managed to come back alive, the country would take care of you."

With that, the vet looked like he was in a trance. His eyes became glassy and he wasn't looking at me anymore, instead he was preaching to the streets, to his past self, to everybody that ever slept on him.

"Don't trust the CIA. Don't ever mess with the

CIA. I called their business line, you know the number, y'all know the number, ladies and gentlemen, the number for the CIA is 703-482-████. Call them and tell them you KNOW they watching you."

People walked by staring at us, but I couldn't tell if they could hear him. Almost everybody was in their own world with their earbuds on, but the vet kept ranting as if he was speaking to millions.

"They sent me to Vietnam, they sent me to do business with Escobar in Colombia, they sent me to make a deal with the Castro boys in Cuba, and now they wanna send me to the Kremlin, but only if they can find me, and that's why you ain't see me!"

"I ain't see you, sir. Don't worry. I gotta get going anyway. God bless."

My words woke him to whatever reality he was in before when we were talking and his gaze sharpened. He started talking different, different enough for me not to feel like leaving immediately anymore.

"When I got back to the states, the first thing I did was buy my mama a new house and my pops a '69 Mustang. Then, I called the bank to buy twenty million nickels, but the Feds hit me up with a billion questions. Reserve boys. Interrogating me about my intentions."

I didn't know what this dude was talking about anymore. I needed a graceful exit.

"Well, sir, it's been real, but I gotta get rolling. My Mama's gonna be waiting. But I just wanna know, like, what's the craziest way you've seen a man die, if you don't mind my asking."

Now before you get all judgmental and tell me I never should have been provoking some homeless PTSD vet on the street, asking him about traumatic memories, you have to understand, I never saw a man die. Most of my friends had. I just acted like I knew what the air tastes like the moment after somebody's soul got snatched. I couldn't walk in my Father's world, earn his respect, until I tasted it. Maybe with enough questions I could fake it without any blood being spilled.

"In a war, youngblood, you see men get shot and step on landmines all day, but there was a time when we were out in the Pacific ice cold water, before we left for Vietnam, and a couple sharks swam circles around me and my best friend. I still don't know how I made it out alive, but I lost my brother that day. I lost my best friend in my own arms. The only thing the lieutenant said to me was something about men containing their grief and something about sharks being around longer than the dinosaurs."

I almost couldn't believe what he was saying, but sometimes you could tell what life had done to someone just by looking at their face. I felt so bad for him.

"My brother used to say, and I'll never forget," he went on. "'If you changed ten lives, and those ten changed another ten, and that happened for five generations, then eight hundred million people would be closer to living their best life.'"

Before I left, the homeless man told me about some connection between prayer and listening and another story about a woman named Henrietta Lacks. He said she was involved with making the Polio vaccine and a whole bunch of other amazing things, but one day she got diagnosed with cancer.

The doctors at John Hopkins, instead of following the protocol, extracted tissue samples for research without her consent, and they discovered something extremely special in her DNA that helped the pharmaceutical industry make billions, but Henrietta's family never got that information for until, like, twenty-five years later when the BBC came out with a documentary.

I walked away from that situation thinking about so many different things and how the world made it seem like poor people had no moral worth, but in all honesty, it's not like wealth automatically made anybody virtuous. I took a few deep breaths, cracked my knuckles, and checked my notifications. Somehow, my battery was still at one percent.

CHAPTER X

Magic City

There was one unread message from Sade. I found out her brother's fiancé was pregnant with their first kid, which was pretty crazy considering Sade's older brother had gotten his legs blown off just a couple weeks after he got to an outpost outside the northern Syrian city of Aburjayla. His fiancé was worried they would never be able to have kids, but one of the military doctors had successfully sewed her brother's balls into his upper thighs right after the explosion. Sade said he earned a Purple Heart.

I still had time, so I decided to swing by the Portrait Gallery to see the Kehinde Wiley and Amy Sherald paintings that Sade had been telling me about. She said everybody was going crazy over the work because Obama and Michelle were the first black people to receive official portraits. I made my way upstairs and waited in a short line to see the Michelle piece, but when I got up front, some dude behind me and his girl were being loud, taking selfies and not even looking at the art.

She started going through filters until he had to take a call. I overheard him say something about handling a lick in Maryland right before we walked out. I couldn't hear everything, and obviously I was missing a lot of the context, but it sounded like Magic City was plotting and scheming, cooking something up as usual, and everybody knew the only major happening in Maryland that Friday night was Sophisticated Ignorance.

Pablo had some friends in Magic City, and he told me they had the kind of money that could keep a small bank on Benning Road from failing. They had about twenty clans in Southeast, dominated some of the most fertile territory, and their small problems always escalated into bloody feuds.

There had been a big story in the local news a few months ago about how one of the recruits got arrested for driving some dudes to rob a pawn shop. They all got caught because the pawn shop owner pulled out a shotgun and started blasting. The driver took a plea deal and snitched his way out of doing time. Some people said he moved out West and entered witness protection, but the Feds found his body a few weeks ago at Whitehall Bay, hanging upside down with his throat slit, a standard Magic City move. Draining bodies made it easier to move them around.

I wasn't even paying attention to the other pieces in the gallery, just shuffling along in line, thinking about what the guy on the phone behind me had said. It had me super paranoid. When I got back to the car, I was thinking through a bunch of different scenarios, wondering if I'd need protection. Luckily, Mama's appointment ran long, giving me time to think in peace.

CHAPTER XI

Science and Miracles

Mama got back to the car around six thirty. She said the doctors needed more blood work before they could give a confident diagnosis. I couldn't read the doctor's cursive handwriting on the prescription, but I knew the drugs wouldn't be able to fix the childhood neglect. I had a feeling she would extend my punishment, or worse, send me to rehab. I was ready to beg for her permission to let me transfer and take my talents somewhere else. There had to be another school that would accept me, especially with my relatively good grades and high test scores.

On the drive back, I thought about how to sneak out and borrow the car. I used to sneak out my bedroom window and climb down the gutter, which was easy during the summertime...but that may not be necessary. If Mama got belligerent and blacked out, I could easily walk right out the back door. I wanted to tell her how much this party meant to me, but she wouldn't get it. She never had a good social life, and I'm not sure what that did to her psychologically, but I was the one facing the long-term consequences.

There was no way I could miss the party. Not seeing my best friends after being expelled made no sense, especially with the possibility of being sent away for a long time. Sade was going to be there, and I wasn't about to miss that opportunity. I didn't know if I was in love or if my mind was on lust lockdown, but it felt like me and Sade were identical souls with a real friendship, and the party was guaranteed to be a treasure house of good memories.

We stopped at a Carry Out on Florida Avenue. I got the usual: chicken fried rice, orange soda, French fries with black pepper and mumbo sauce. When we got back home, Mama parked on the driveway. It being such a quiet night, you could hear the frozen layer on top of the snow crunch and pop like bubble wrap under our feet.

I took my shoes off by the door, carried the food

into the kitchen, and set the table. Mama dove into her box of wine. I had seen those patterns before and quite often. That was her poison and I used to wonder if anyone else had parents going through the same thing. The doctors said the brain of an addict changed forever and there was no way it could go back, but Mama was too stubborn to listen. Everybody has their stubborn attachments these days.

She answered a call and I could tell it was Uncle Roy. We used to play basketball in DuPont and rollerblade down the Pennsylvania Avenue bike lanes. I didn't see him too often, especially not after Yolanda caught him. Some people said she was the one who hired the guys from Magic City to rob his condo.

Uncle Roy had come back home early from a trip and walked in on two dudes wearing ski masks stealing his safe around two in the morning. They shot him in the leg twice, but somehow, he managed to get his gun from under the mattress and fire back. Later on, his leg had to be amputated and replaced with a prosthetic. The cops had zero leads and never found the shooters.

Mama left the room, still talking to Uncle Roy, and I sat down to eat by myself while the rest of the family came trickling in, one by one. After finishing dinner, I hung out in the living room longer than usual, hoping that by hanging around longer my family wouldn't be suspicious of me disappearing later. My sister was playing the piano and my Grandma had been sitting on her favorite chair, holding my baby brother. Diamond was obsessed with music and she could talk to you for hours about all kinds of weird stuff like the frequency of two keys on a piano being six percent apart or whatever. Grandma loved listening to her play, especially after being diagnosed with Alzheimer's.

My brother and I did our new handshake and he didn't mess it up. He would usually struggle to raise his arms, mainly because of a problem in his brain that made it hard for him to move. Sometimes it seemed like the only thing he could do was smile, laugh, or cry. The doctors used to say he would never be able to walk or get out of bed without help...but they also used to say that nobody could reverse diabetes, and that ended up being wrong. So, who knows what's possible—maybe science and miracles aren't mutually exclusive.

CHAPTER XII

My Father's Gun (8PM)

I went to grab the pistol from my safe spot and didn't remember that Zanie still had it until my hand grabbed nothing but air. When my head got all full of noise and stress, like today, I forgot the most essential pieces. Zanie would usually never hold a gun for me but she changed her mind after I told her the alternative was me being shipped out West with no phone privileges. I learned early on from watching my parents that love tempts us to abandon boundaries.

I had never lost track of the gun ever since I got it last summer, through one of Pablo's friends, Dimitri. I remembered the day I'd gotten it; the way Dimitri had called me by my real name. Even though everybody knew me as X, Dimitri would call me Elon, which was weird because nobody else did that, except my family. I flopped on my bed and pulled out my phone, scrolling and clicking without thinking while I waited for my family to go to bed.

My Father gave me the middle name X after Malcolm because he knew that peace and love were weak protection against the evil of the world he knew so well. Mama would always argue with him and often quote MLK. She said everybody deserves compassion and that hate couldn't drive out hate. She had a point, but a loving, peaceful person is still just as dead when his enemy puts a bullet in his head. But there was no way Sean King or anybody from Magic City would pull up and catch me off guard tonight.

I'd made Zanie hold my gun last weekend when Mama was going through my internet history and emptying out my pockets. She was trying to get some undeniable proof that I needed military school. When Mama popped off like that I knew she had been stressing out about my Father, feeling like she was failing at parenting a teenage boy on her own. I'm sure every time she saw me, she remembered him. Mama used to get really drunk and say my father didn't come around that often because he was ashamed of me. Truth be told, she was right —but with him away, I was writing my own rules, without honest feedback and no long-term thinking.

I must've fallen asleep, because I suddenly jerked awake and it was late. I walked into the bathroom, brushed my teeth, dabbed myself with my father's cologne, and tiptoed downstairs. I looked good and my father always used to say, "You should dress as if you'll be murdered in those clothes." All the lights were off in the living room. Everybody must have been knocked out. Mama was toasted on the couch holding a bottle of brown liquor and *Dreams from My Father*.

I stuck her feet inside the blanket and moved the bottle and the book to the coffee table. I adjusted her neck, but I was gentle enough not to wake her. Before I left her side, I said a little prayer and I wondered if my dad did stuff like that before he left. Grandma was talking in her sleep about tea with milk and a radio transistor on the gold chair. I went into my father's closet and tested out combinations to his safe.

Azmi Abusam

CHAPTER XIII

Stay Woke

I connected my phone to the aux and stuck the key in the ignition. After checking the mirrors and disengaging the break, I fed the car gas and turned down 49th to scoop up Grayson. The snow was coming down pretty heavy and you could barely see anything in front of you. I was riding dirty so I had to be extra cautious. When I pulled up to Grayson's house, I remember seeing his silhouette through the living room window.

Grayson became more depressed after his parents got divorced and his mom married a racist man who couldn't get over her dancing. To be honest, I was worried about his depression and anxiety making him overdose. I think he felt like his mom's past was his fault, and the way she was getting emotionally abused by his stepdad was all his fault too. I knew he was really going through it but I told him no amount of weed would iron out his issues. He didn't take that very well, but I was just being honest.

The last time he came out with us, he got wasted and was almost arrested for choking out some dude. Before I could think about all the crazy stuff he might do that night at SI, he jogged to the car and jumped in. I remember that conversation pretty well because I was so paranoid about him smelling so loud.

"Yo! I hope you got some cologne," I said. "We don't need the car smelling like anything but these Little Christmas Trees."

"Chill, dog," said Grayson. "Yo mama ain't gone smell nothing. I got a bottle right here."

"It ain't just about my Mama, stupid. If we get pulled over and a cop gets a whiff, we're done. I mean, you might get off being half white, but I'd be lucky to make it out alive."

"You mad paranoid, dog, and if we get pulled over, I'm playing up this whiteness and getting us off with a warning."

"I guess what's the point of having advantages and not using them," I laughed.

"Exactly, dog, one of my cousins almost got locked up the other day on H Street. Cops had him pressed up against the cruiser, handcuffed and everything because he was driving on a suspended. But he finessed his way out the situation by knowing how to talk that talk."

"Eloquence is knowing when to shut up, I mean, ain't that what Jeezy said?"

"*Thug Motivation* still goes hard, dog," said Grayson. "But now we got rappers acting like trappers, but they're probably just workaholics, locking themselves up in the studio making bangers."

"They probably have to make a hundred songs just to find ten good ones. I was just talking to shorty about this the other day, and she was saying some of the best art just grows out of necessity."

"Dog, people forget being an artist is a burden, but since everybody's born unfree and unequal, you ain't got no choice but to accept the fate, even if that means no big rewards."

"Speaking of rewards, guess who got the new GTA codes, bruh? Did you see my new all glass beach house in Malibu with the bulletproof Teslas sitting outside?"

"Ooh wee!" Grayson said. "Send me the link, like, ASAP."

"I spent so much money last night on this all white Lamborghini, the same one Leonardo had in the *Wolf of Wall Street*."

"The white 1989 Lamborghini Countach," Grayson said. "That was the real car in the movie too. The producers were obsessed with everything being real. And if you ask me, my mans Leo deserved an Oscar, but obviously the Academy's been robbing some actors. Reverse racism, dog. Hashtag: Oscars getting too black. Stay woke, boy."

"You've been killing way too many brain cells, bro. You should stop drinking and smoking cuz you sound stupid. Oh, by the way, I ran into Ava and Veronica today when we got out."

"What?" Grayson spluttered. "That should've been the first thing you said to me! So...did she ask about me?"

"Naw, not at all. But they're going to the party tonight and they want us to bring tequila."

"I ain't bringing them nothing," said Grayson. "Roni wants to act like it's over, but she's still sending me late night texts, and I know she's only interested in me because I look like a snack. But that's why I let her know if she can't handle me at my worst, she doesn't deserve me at my best."

I laughed at him and thought about Zanie and

how she could handle me at my worst and help me improve my best. I didn't dwell on her though, I couldn't take any more negative thoughts. I was gonna be on my worst behavior that night, but I knew I could earn her forgiveness. I kept driving towards Amir's house and playing armchair psychologist to Grayson.

"You need to move on and date somebody else," I said. "That's how you get over somebody. Look that up if you don't believe me. I mean, obviously, most people you meet won't be compatible, especially if you have high standards, but there's somebody out there looking for you."

"Easier said than done, bro," said Grayson. "But you seem to be getting real compatible with Sade...is she gonna be there tonight?"

"I feel like she wants me, but I don't want that drama. But look, we're blessed, bro, we're some young, handsome dudes and there's nine billion fish in the sea."

"I just can't believe I was stupid enough to fall for her, especially that night at the pool when we came back from the concert," said Grayson. "My moms heard us that night and Roni's so wild, instead of leaving, she made us go into the garage. That's how I got that big scar on my leg."

"But Roni wasn't with you shooting in the gym. She's still curious about getting attention from hot dudes. She isn't ready to be loyal. The truth hurts, but I can't lie to you."

"I'd rather hear the truth," said Grayson. "I don't need therapeutic friends gassing me up with lies and fake tales."

"Yup...and that's why they say, 'A loyal woman is better than a pretty face.'"

"Dog, why can't we have both?" Grayson said. "And is that Sade who keeps blowing up your phone? You bout to have a good night homie, but then again, that crazy ex of hers is probably gonna be there surveilling."

CHAPTER XIV

Like a Snack

We pulled up to Pablo's spot and I saw him in the garage arguing with his stepfather. The garage door was about two thirds of the way open. His biological dad was doing time for mortgage fraud. Pablo was pretty private about the whole thing, but we all knew.

Grayson scrolled through my Spotify and asked me about Zanie, but I changed the subject and talked about something else. I didn't have time to think about that situation. I also didn't feel like thinking about what would happen if Mama saw the car missing, the possibility of running into Sean and his dumb yes men at the party, or getting caught with my father's strap.

Grayson rolled down his window and we heard Pablo saying something about Kobe and Westbrook being two of the best players of all time. His step-father said something about LeBron and Jordan and players not caving in. It was hard to catch everything, but then Pablo went off about players being unapologetic when exercising their freedom to move around. He said something about them chasing a ring or a check, and at some point, everybody had to think about life after basketball, especially after giving a city or a company your prime years.

I drove slowly around Benning Road because of all the speed cameras and we ran into a detour by H Street. I thought it was a police checkpoint at first and my pulse was pounding like crazy, but it turned out to just be three old ladies standing behind crime scene tape, talking to the cops.

We drove by two female police officers who gawked right at me and I don't know why they didn't pull us over immediately, but I'm sure it had something to do with me sitting up straight and grabbing the steering wheel with two hands like my Grandma was driving.

"That cop was checking you out, E! Turn back around and get that number, dog!" Amir said.

"Officer Kurechi looking at you like a snack!" Grayson said. "Maybe she wanna take you in...show you why Black Lives Matter."

These dudes were in the mood to joke around, but all that nonsense did nothing to calm my paranoia. For a second, I thought twelve was on to us. I kept checking the rearview, but nobody was on our tail. Then, I took my eyes off the road for a split second and a crackhead sprinted out of a 7-Eleven.

The car in front of us slammed on their brakes to avoid him and fishtailed, so that I had to swerve off the road so I didn't ram into his bumper. Nobody got hurt and the car seemed fine, but it shook my nerves even more and led to a few wrong turns. We got off 295 early and drove a few miles until we passed the Shakespeare Theatre and some hotel.

"Yo...that's the spot where MLK gave that 'I Have a Dream' speech," said Amir. "Real talk."

I was looking for a parking spot when four college-aged looking girls pulled up next to us in a black Jeep at the red light by the Chinatown sign. Grayson and Amir rolled the windows down, spit some game, and swapped Instagram handles with the driver and one of the girls sitting in the back.

They were spazzing out when I pulled off, celebrating the interaction, and I was so happy to see the same homeless Vietnam vet I'd met earlier sitting under the Capital One arena billboard, building a tent out of newspaper and lost umbrellas.

I parked the car outside a sushi restaurant, and Grayson and I walked up to the vet and began negotiating like we had been at Camp David. The homeless man asked for more money than we expected and he rambled about some special counsel investigation, but ultimately we made a sweet deal, and thirty minutes later, as soon as we started arguing about whether or not we got finessed, the man came back bearing gifts. The look on Pablo and Amir's face when we got back to the car was priceless.

"Yo, tonight's about to be the best night ever," said Pablo.

"We really just pulled that off, huh," said Amir. "I swear life a movie, bro—tonight we on a whole new vibe, bruh, a whole new wave—"

"I feel like a divine mission has just been accomplished, dog," said Grayson.

"Let's not get carried away," I said. "We still gotta get there."

There wasn't much traffic once we got deeper into Maryland and the rest of the ride went by smoothly. Right before midnight, the GPS took us off the highway and sent us down some narrow, winding back roads leading up to a mansion that was sitting on a cliff that immediately fell to the frozen lake below. The closest neighbors must have been a few miles away. The moonlight hit the ice in a way that gave off a beautiful glow. I turned the engine off and said alhamdulillah—thanking God for keeping us alive.

Grayson was riding shotgun, filling up his vintage camera flask with tequila. Pablo was in the back seat stuffing things into his backpack and Amir was cake baking on the phone. I wondered if Sade was already inside. I didn't see her Nissan.

As soon as we got out, Pablo's friend Dimitri pulled up next to us in a little silver Jetta. He was wearing too many gold chains and waving a cigarette out the window. His energy was weird to me and he had strange manners. Dimitri's girlfriend got out the car eyeing down Grayson. She gave me a hug and I could tell she was wearing the same Tiffany perfume I gave Zanie for her birthday. Pablo, who was entirely unsuspicious of Dimitri, started talking to him like they were best friends.

The rest of us walked up to the property and found a massive line out front. We waited for a few minutes until somebody got a hold of Veronika and Ava. They pulled us out of line; they had extra gold VIP bracelets, and they got us in much faster through the back. We climbed up a spiral staircase that put us on the balcony of the third floor, overlooking the indoor pool and the bottom two floors of the other wing.

CHAPTER XV

Love Isn't Chess

The party was so ridiculously indescribable Shakespeare would've had trouble finding the words to write a poem about it. I took a second to look around and absorb everything. The house was furnished with more style than I had ever seen and it was flooded with so many beautiful people rocking their best outfits, holding red cups filled to the brim, singing, laughing, dancing super provocatively, living their best life, and the music was fire. Somebody told me that the DJ's, twin brothers on the spectrum, could see sounds like Pharell.

At that moment, I understood why people said, "relationships were born out of SI." The living room had rich-colored rugs and you could tell the place was custom designed from top to bottom. The spot had gorgeous photographs against a Hague Blue wall, huge mount faux antlers, and oversized letters spelling out the word "LOVE" in many languages. I overheard one girl saying all of the pieces were carefully curated by the designer Habachy.

The guys and I made our way into the kitchen and I remember seeing Ava and Veronika by the ice maker wearing twinning outfits. They added the coincidence to their Instagram Story and gave me credit for taking the shot, then introduced us to some super fine sisters from a rival high school. Ava knew them from some dance competition.

We shared our drinks and snacks and somehow, we got on the subject of addiction. Somebody said it wasn't that serious, which didn't make any sense to me, but then again, nobody knew about Mama's situation. Most likely, she wasn't going to wake up until my father got back home.

One of the girls asked me to make her a drink and she ended up being very chatty. Apparently, she moved up to D.C. a few years ago; her dad's job brought him out here, and the whole family moved. He was making documentaries and he wanted her to follow in his footsteps, but she was all about launching a beauty company and making lip gloss like Kylie. I kept talking to her, even though I was distracted thinking about Sade. Luckily, I got reunited with the guys a few minutes later.

Grayson ate more of the baked brisket wreath dip and said, "The movies from the '90s might be old, but there's endless classics. I just saw a really good one on Netflix the other day—I forgot the name, but it's about a dude who gets a second apartment and lets his friends use it to hang out with their secretaries...but it's super old and it's in black and white."

"People be sleeping on the old stuff, but you have to spin each album twice to know if it's really good," Amir said.

Grayson took one of the fried mashed potatoe balls off my plate and said, "Y'all ever heard of a Hollywood film festival in Cuba? I got an email yesterday saying I won two tickets. I think it might be legit since Cuba's legal and everything."

Pablo laughed. "Sounds like the time you got an offer from the West African Bernie Madoff. Did he ever help you double your money?"

"Nah, it sounds like the Frye Festival, to be honest," Ava said. "Please don't get robbed falling for that fake news...dudes will fall for anything these days."

"But this might be different," Pablo said. "Claim those tickets and take me as a wingman. I heard they got some of the most striking women of all time."

"The real queens live in East Africa, bro," Amir said. "Didn't I send y'all a photo of the half-East African and half-British girl?"

"Man, somebody told me the Cubans have every look," said Grayson. "From white, blue eyes, and blond hair to chocolate brown, dark eyes, dark hair."

"I think that girl from Univision is Cuban," I said. "I mean, she might be something else, but all I know is Aaliyah and Angelina Jolie are some of the most beautiful women of all time."

"Aaliyah all naturally beautiful," said Pablo. "Ain't nothing wrong with getting work, but organic is better than genetically modified."

"They don't make them like that no more either!" Grayson said.

"Yeah they do, but y'all don't know where to look," Amir said. "You ain't gon' find nothing doing all that swiping. Now it's about meeting someone organically and being real—love ain't chess."

"We need a trip to Amsterdam," Grayson said. "They're off the charts and I heard they're speaking like four different languages fluently."

"Man, we need to hit up Africa," Pablo said. "Or go to one of those Richard Branson islands where him and Obama and Jay Z kick it and smoke Cubans—"

Amir saved his drink from falling and said, "Once you're on Richard Branson island, bro...that's when you know you made it."

"Speaking of Jay Z, y'all need to see the Kalief Browder documentary Hov made," I said. "This dude did about three years at Rikers. Solitary confinement. Kept pushing his trial back. Eventually, after he got out, I think it was so hard for him to readjust, he killed himself."

These guys were already too wasted to think about someone like us dying, much less take down my movie recommendations, so I got myself another drink and scanned the room for Sade.

"Man...y'all boys stupid—Paris is where we need to be," said Grayson. "Know y'all seen Alicia Aylies...Miss France. That's why I'm on this 'Bonjour, Mademoiselle.' Do y'all even know what I just said?"

"She ain't no Marpessa Dawn though!" Amir said. "That woman was beyond beauty."

Some of the girls next to us had been arguing about fashion running in cycles and some of the guys on the other side were watching the videos playing on the projector and arguing about Leonardo da Vinci working with the Medici family. I was drifting in and out of the conversation, barely paying attention. I stopped paying attention completely when I saw the same dude from the Art Gallery walk through the doors wearing a fur-collared leather. His buddy was wearing a multi-colored ski jacket and they were acting funny but I tried not to pay them any attention.

CHAPTER XVI

Twerking Inside My Heart

Hearing French made me think about Josephine Baker. My father once said that she created and then destroyed some stereotypes about black people. This was a girl who had been born into poverty in St. Louis and quit school at thirteen to start dancing but went on to become this celebrity who used her status to push forward the civil rights movement.

It takes courage to be a real dream chaser. My father told me all this when I found the poster of her wearing nothing but a banana skirt, and he said that he'd had it hanging up in his dorm room back in the day. His homeboy Ernest used to say she was "the most sensational woman anyone ever saw." I wondered what her Instagram page would look like.

She moved to Paris and got super famous but when she came back home to America, the racism and ignorance kept people from understanding her value and her contribution, so she decided to live in France and went back. Still, she came back later just to support the Civil Rights movement and marched with MLK in D.C. and everything. I added more sticky chicken wings to my plate and zoned back into the conversation.

"I just want an IG model but first I gotta grow out my beard and keep drinking this vitamin water," Grayson said.

Amir scoffed. "I don't even wanna end up with a ten, brother—I just need a good chick with a good job who's more religious for the balance."

"Yeah, yeah, we know," Pablo snickered. "A girl who's gonna help you improve your relationship with the Lord—keep you on the right path—you geeking."

"You know that's a lie," Grayson said.

Ava rolled her eyes and folded her arms in front of her. "All you boys think about is basketball, playing video games, and dating foreign women. Y'all can't see long term...y'all can't even see beyond two or three years into the future. That's probably too hard for a man's brain."

Grayson laughed loudly at that. "Guilty! I ain't gon' lie."

"You just mad 'cause you never had anybody love you," Pablo said.

"Boy, bye—I don't need a man to make me feel like my life is complete, especially not a lame boy like you with no ambition," Ava snapped back.

"At least I don't look like Freddy Kruger," Pablo said.

"Boy, I know you ain't talking...that's why you look like a giraffe and elephant had a baby!" Ava said.

"Y'all argue about dumb stuff too much," I said, drawn into the conversation when Amir and Grayson started cackling at the offended look on Pablo's face. "That's why my mans Shakespeare used to say there's nothing good or bad—people just be giving things meaning."

"Bruh, did y'all know Shakespeare worked on the King James Version of the Bible?" Grayson said.

"That's fake news, bruh," Amir said.

"Nah, for real. They say if you go to Psalm 46 and count forty-six words forward, you find Shake, and if you count forty-six words backwards, you find Speare—and that version got published in 1610, when Shakespeare was forty-six years old...the clues all around us but y'all ain't woke. Y'all sleep-walking. Wokeness percolating."

"What were you saying about Fetty Wap last week?" Pablo said.

Grayson suddenly got really excited. "Well, y'all know Fetty Wap represent 1738, right?"

"Duh, bro. Who doesn't know that?"

"Well, that's 5:38 in military time. Fetty five letters. Wap three. But if you add it up, it's eight, and Matthew 5:38 is 'an eye for an eye' and Fetty ain't got no eye...so he must be Illuminati," Grayson said triumphantly.

I rolled my eyes at him and tuned out the conversation again. Speaking of missing eyes had me thinking of my father and what he'd say to me this coming Sunday when I saw him. Hopefully nothing too bad. This heavy glock needed to be back in the safe, tucked in like a little baby.

I looked around the crowded room, feeling extra agitated. There was still no sign of Sade or Sean. Were they together somewhere? Pablo was next to me having a serious conversation with some girl wearing little blue Ugg boots, jeans, a Fashionova hoodie, and glasses. She was talking about how you should get to know somebody well before dating them.

I checked my phone. Zanie sent me a couple text messages around that time, but I didn't check them because right then I noticed Sade walking up to me from across the room in a tight red dress. She smiled, winked at me and moved her finger, beckoning me to walk over to her. I did, and she gave me a big, juicy hug.

"Elon! I'm glad you decided to come out. When did you get here? I've been looking all over for you. You didn't even open my snaps yet," she fake pouted the last part.

"I just got here not too long ago...you look really good. How long have you been here?"

"I don't even know anymore because we drank so much at the pregame—honestly, my liver has to be the size of a beach ball at this point. Jell-O shots delicious, can't resist...no, can't resist," she whispered the last bit in my ear.

She looked really good that night and we'd never been this drunk together. "I've already lost track of how many I've had so I know I'm gonna be super hungover tomorrow," I laughed.

There was a projector inside one of the living rooms playing some old classic Marilyn Monroe movie and I was so drunk I didn't know what else to talk about.

"You ever seen this?"

She grinned. "Boy, I've been following Marilyn Monroe ever since she was in the first issue of *Playboy*. This is *Gentlemen Prefer Blondes*."

"Yeah, she's really good and I always thought she deserved more serious roles. She was more versatile than people thought...the same thing happened to the dude who played Sherlock Holmes for twelve years and they say he was a classically trained Shakespearian actor and everything." I didn't know too much about Marilyn but wanted Sade to do all the talking. I was having to focus extremely hard to keep my attention on the conversation and to keep my words from slurring at all.

Sade nodded. "Such an Earth angel...it sucks how an actress can get typecast and people never get a chance to see the full spectrum of her talent, and people don't think enough about how hard it is for someone to experience fame and keep the same sense of contentment."

I found myself saying something about how she'd keep me content and touched the gold Sade necklace on her chest and we kept flirting for a while. She had several necklaces on; the other necklace resembled an abstract moon. When the DJs played some new songs from the Wale and Kendrick album, I saw Sean standing on a couch across the living room with a strange smile on his face.

Some other Magic City dudes were on the dancefloor close to him holding Styrofoam cups, doing gang dances. Sade and I kept talking and dancing and I could tell she noticed them, but she pretended like nothing changed. I assumed she didn't want to make Sean jealous, so we went upstairs where the vibe was more chill and nobody noticed us because everybody was low-key getting freaky too.

Azmi Abusam

CHAPTER XVII

Honey Lamb Hood Booger

Half an hour later, the DJs finally looked out for all of us and switched to slow jams by Luther Vandross. Sade grabbed my hand and led me through the crowd gracefully and even though it felt like we were completely alone, I wondered if anyone from Magic City had seen us slip out. I'm usually mad perceptive, but once I've been drinking and smoking, it's too hard for me to see reality.

I double-checked my pocket to make sure everything was still there. The last thing I needed was Sade getting knocked up, especially because after that night, I had plans to hibernate with Zanie. She was the one for that; the one who would keep me out of trouble. Keep me from failing and being sent away to military school.

Sade took me upstairs to the third floor and we accidentally walked in on Grayson and Veronica making out, but the second bedroom was empty. She jumped on me as soon as we entered the room and wrapped her legs around my waist. Her short tight dress slipped up and she was feeling all over me, but me being so wasted, I lost my balance and fell backwards onto the bed.

I was in a habit of hiding my gun with Zanie before we started doing anything (even though she'd always notice), but I knew Sade was the kind of girl who'd love it being right out on the nightstand. I slipped it out and it landed with a smack on the smooth surface. She let out a thrilled giggle and we went back to kissing.

She kept her red bottom heels on, looking better than the models in the Victoria's Secret catalogue. That's when I realized all those emojis, mixed signals, and flirting wasn't my vanity; she was without a doubt extremely into me. She had a slight smile on her face, and I could tell she was trying to read my mind but right before things got very heated my phone started vibrating in my pocket.

I tried to ignore the calls, but whoever it was

kept calling back. I knew it had to be Amir or Pablo because Grayson was all tied up. Didn't they know better than to bother me right now? After three or four calls, Sade pulled the phone from my pocket before I could grab her hand just like a sexy ninja pickpocket.

She saw "Honey Lamb Hood Booger" on the caller ID above Zanie's hottest selfie and sat straight up and launched the phone at the headboard with a rage. The impact left a dent in the soft wood of the headboard but thank God my phone wasn't cracked. I scrambled upright to retrieve it from where it had clattered to the floor. Sade was livid, throwing a tantrum and screaming at me...leaving me with no choice but to put my clothes back on and go outside to check in with Zanie.

"It's not what it looks like so don't even go making all those stupid assumptions like you know what you're talking about, because you don't," I snapped at her. "You need to calm down throwing my phone like that—who do you think you are?"

"Go be with Zanie! She's such a goody goody, good luck getting her to satisfy you the way I can. You need to choose who you wanna be with, E! I ended things with Sean and I'm working my ass off to make you happy. My whole world could be about you, and you're out here making me look dumb when you obviously haven't ended things with that girl!"

"Look, calm down," I put my hands on her arms and tried to soothe her. "I don't know why she's calling me, but I already let her know it's over. I wanna be with you...you know this. Loyalty is everything and you know I don't feel like myself unless I'm making you happy. Okay? Lemme just find out what's going on 'cause I got too many missed calls from her and my folks. But stay right here and lock the door."

"You need to hurry up and bring me back some water and snacks," she huffed, flopping down on the bed and glaring at me. "And if you ain't back in five minutes, you won't find me."

"Aight...just chill, I'll be right back. Don't go nowhere."

CHAPTER XVIII

Airplane Mode

On my way to the front door, I saw some Magic City dudes on the white leather sofas in the parlor, dancing and throwing up sets with a whole gaggle of girls twerking for Patron shots. I prayed nobody would get pregnant. Sean wasn't with them and I stepped outside onto the driveway. The freezing air cleared my head a little, though everything looked like it was moving slower than it should have. I had missed calls from almost everybody; Zanie, Mama, even my father, and for some reason, they all had left voicemails... which was weird because they usually never did that.

Outside, you would've sworn it was the Russian

tundra, but you could still hear the bass bumping and see people blowing smoke out the windows.

One dude was on the edge of the balcony getting ready to jump off, probably thinking he could fly, but his friends were trying to talk him out of it. I didn't know him well, but I saw him earlier pouring syrup into a spoon and spreading it inside a blunt he was rolling. His entire crew had been snorting powder, popping X pills, and adding Jolly Ranchers and Skittles to their drinks. I thought about Gucci Mane after his transformation.

In the first voice message, my father was yelling so hard I could barely understand him. He said something about the Impala and not finding his glock. At that point I was so toasted that I thought once I got home he'd be proud of me for breaking into the safe since I really needed something. Anyway, all I did was plug in everybody's date of birth and use the process of elimination until it popped open. He either thought I was dumb, or he wanted me to be able to get inside in case of an emergency.

I didn't even go through all the stuff. There was some brand-new iPhones, business cards, and a ton of crispy hundred-dollar bills in a small bag. I didn't touch the money. Mama always said, "God sees everything."

Zanie had sent me text messages in all caps saying Mama forced her to give up my location, which really pissed me off since she'd promised she would never do that. She said the cops were looking for me too because I had been reported missing, which freaked me out. I switched to airplane mode, even though it probably didn't make a difference. I figured the snowstorm would slow the Feds down and buy me time to sober up, at least.

To be honest, I was so gone, I thought I could go back upstairs and take care of business with Sade, drop the guys off at home and then go crash with Zanie. I knew if I drove straight home, more than likely, the Feds would find me, and I'd probably get shot.

CHAPTER XIX

Jealousy

I broke the seal by a big tree behind the mansion, and Grayson and Amir found me outside through the Find My Friends app. They were going on about Pablo being MIA and things getting rowdy inside. Apparently, some drama popped off and some folks started fighting. I knew things were serious when I saw some guys by the side of the house walk to their cars and grab bats out of the trunk.

The three of us went back in together and looked for Pablo on every floor, but he was nowhere to be found. If it was a regular night, I would have continued to look for him, but I had more important things to do. I let Grayson and Amir keep searching

—I had to get back to Sade. At this point, the party was flooded with people and the house had to be two or three times over capacity. The dance floors were still packed - you couldn't take a step without bumping into somebody...and everyone was yelling at the top of their lungs as if it was their last night on Earth. I needed to take a number two but the bathrooms had a long line and girls were peeing right next to dudes throwing up in the sink with the door wide open, and for some reason, that made me crave Taco Bell.

Although my mind was blurry from the alcohol, I was on a mission. I pushed my way through the mayhem. Sade was expecting me to return, and I knew she was far too drunk to leave. I went into the kitchen, grabbed some water bottles, thinking I had been gone for less than five minutes, but on my way up the spiral stairs I heard loud banging on a bedroom door, and I unmistakably heard my name be called. The voice was so steady, deep, and nasty that even my drunk mind jumped to the most dreaded conclusion.

I thought it was the alcohol playing tricks on me for a second, but when I got closer to the top steps, I saw Sean in his red Helly Hanson kicking in the door and pulling out a Glock 17 holstered under the small of his back. Then, right after, Sade screamed, somebody opened fire, and the music immediately stopped. The abrupt silence after the deafening noise of the party made my ears ring. Then, ten more shots in rapid succession and everyone was screaming and running downstairs with their hands over their heads like an active shooter drill, and I ran to the closest doorway.

Sean came out of the room I'd left Sade in a couple seconds later; he had been shot in the left leg. Three of his boys carried him away. One of his boys, who was carrying a multifaceted knife, hit the wall face-first. His nose shattered and he cracked his head when he fell back. I pushed past multiple people fighting and throwing chairs and running in the opposite direction and lurched into the room.

Nothing could have prepared me for what I saw.

Sade was sitting up in the bed where I left her, alive but in shock, quivering and naked with a pistol sitting next to her. There was a nickel-sized gash on top of her left eye and blood trickled down her face. But she wasn't looking at me—she was staring at Pablo, where he lay on the floor.

My friend was on the ground, pretty much naked too, with multiple gunshot wounds. Some of the bullets must have gone through his aorta or one of those big veins because the blood was flowing out freely and so much of the tissue was gone. The entry points weren't as big as the exit wounds and a few shots must have landed in his spleen or maybe one of his kidneys. He was moving feebly, somehow still alive.

I couldn't comprehend everything I was seeing, and I felt like I was about to blackout. I got one of those throw up burps and some food came up but I swallowed it back down. However, my stomach wasn't able to take the gruesome scene in front of me, so, I threw up a few seconds later and the vomit and the blood on the floor mingled.

People were still screaming and running around, some people now standing in the doorway watching us. Mechanically, without thinking, I picked Sade's dress up off of the floor and used it like gauze to pack some of the bleeding and close part of Pablo's abdomen. Her dress had been next to five or six empty 9mm shells.

Pablo must have been in shock. You could tell his heart wasn't able to pump enough blood, and with each beat, more blood ebbed between my fingers, the fabric of the dress already soaked and useless. His esophagus had to be ruptured.

Our eyes met, and the jealousy I'd felt at finding

him there faded a little, but then his eyes glazed over and I knew he couldn't see me anymore. Jealousy, a really very horrible disease in the heart, was more cruel than death. This was not someplace I needed to be, but if I didn't find my father's gun, he could be charged with two counts of first-degree murder and possibly executed.

CHAPTER XX

A Disease in the Heart

I cut the lights on, checked the nightstand, the dresser, under the bed—but it wasn't there. I searched the room up and down, and checked the closet too, but nothing came up. Sean must have taken it or moved it somewhere else, but I didn't have time to think because the Feds were on their way. I got outta there, but I had to force my way past the people crowded in the doorway of the bedroom. Every single one of them saw my face. Before I left, I got on the bed and started shaking Sade, who was crying silently now, and that's how I got her blood on my hands.

"Sade! Listen to me. Sean did this. Not me," I yelled in her face, grabbing her chin and forcing her face towards mine, staring deeply into her panic ridden eyes. "I need you to remember that when the cops get here. Matter fact, why would you let Pablo in here? What did you do...just don't say nothing about me! You don't even know me, OK? You probably can't even hear me! God dammit!"

Now, before you say I'm guilty for not helping Sade, you have to understand that she was a major liability at that point, and she had just gone behind my back and gotten my best friend murdered. She wasn't going to tell me the truth about Pablo's end. The whole situation was wrapped in utter mystery, but I remembered my father telling me there's some people in this world who would risk their lives just to ruin somebody else's.

I got outside and ran to the car. The snow was dotted with blood and countless girls were panicking, sobbing, and calling their parents. The first super storm of the season intensified outside. Grayson and Amir were already there, waiting for me, despite the danger we were in.

"Yo! What took you so long? Did you find Pablo?" Grayson demanded, his eyes taking in the blood that covered my hands, arms, and clothes.

"Pablo ain't coming, and y'all better find a different ride. Y'all can't come with me. We gotta split up."

"What do you mean?" Amir started to look frantic. "Open the doors before I punch you right now!"

I tried to push past them to get to the driver's door, but Grayson grabbed the sleeve of my shirt and jerked me around to face him. "Dude! What happened upstairs? Did you see what happened?"

"Look," I snarled, shoving him away roughly. "I ain't saying this again; y'all ain't rolling with me, so back up and find another ride!"

They were cussing me out, but I ignored them. Their lives would've been ruined if the police caught them with me. I jumped in the car, locked the doors, and never looked back. I never did them dirty, but it's crazy how easily past kindness is forgotten.

I drove straight to Zanie's spot. Surprisingly, I made it there without crashing, but I have no memories of the drive. All that I could remember was pulling over at a random 7-Eleven, busting open a lighter with a small box cutter and dousing my jacket with the fluid before setting it on fire. It was covered in blood.

Within a matter of minutes, the night had become a symbol of my feckless ignorance, but I knew if I was in Pablo's place, Sean would've been the one

with the bullet in his head. I couldn't stop thinking about how drunk everybody had been. Why was
Pablo in there? Would Sade have any memory if she
survived?

CHAPTER XXI

Spotlight (3AM)

I couldn't believe I made it to Zanie's spot without dying. She opened the basement door without saying a single word to me and her face wrinkled up like she could smell death on me. She looked like the most beautiful woman in the world.

"I should've listened to you," I said, and a sob caught in my throat. "I'm such a stupid idiot for not listening to you."

"I thought you actually loved me," She said. "Didn't I tell you to stay home? Didn't you promise to take me to the movies? But your lips do nothing but tell lies...white lies, my ass. I knew this was too good to be true. But I was stupid enough to forgive you. Every single time. For so many wrongs—"

It felt impossible to speak. I stood there in front of Zanie with the words stuck in my throat. The illusion of everything being okay had disappeared. I was having flashbacks to Sade bleeding out. If she lost a pint of blood she would be dead. Why would Sean kill her? Or was it Pablo? Who stole my father's gun?

It felt like I was going crazy as all of these questions swarmed my head. I needed my therapist. I needed help controlling my thoughts. My therapist knew how to calm me down, but she must've been under oath to report everything to the Feds, so even this was something I would have to deal with on my own.

Zanie was still talking. "...I gave you real love. Utter loyalty. For what? For no reason! You're too dumb and blind to see my worth—"

"Look—I messed up real bad tonight. I'm so stupid. I'm in a really bad place. Sade might be dead, Pablo is dead, and I lost my father's gun—if the cops find it, you know they'll send him back to jail and I can't—"

"I don't believe anything you say," said Zanie. "I don't know who you are anymore. I don't have time to waste with somebody who can't be loyal. My family is fighting for their life in Sudan...fighting for their freedom."

The lump in my throat felt like it was choking me. I got an overwhelming desire to cry, and just like that, tears started rolling down. I felt like the most neglected orphan in the universe and the only thing I could do was cover my face with my shirt. I remembered my mom lecturing me about listening to the ones who make you cry, not the ones who make you laugh. Tonight, I needed to be with somebody who loved me. My family and Zanie were the ones who truly cared about me, and I had been too stupid to see it until now.

"All you do is say empty words and blame your father for your mistakes," She said. "You don't love me, Elon, but God knows all your secrets even if you don't make them known to me—I'm not letting you in unless you tell me everything—are you even capable of that?"

I was running out of time and my head was spinning with thoughts of the worst possible scenarios. All I could do was nod; my throat was still too choked up for words. She stared at me for a few more long seconds, and I could tell she was deciding whether to believe me or not. Finally, she pulled me into a tight hug.

It's too much for me to remember everything Zanie said in that moment—the expression on her face is hard to put into words. But I'll never forget her tears rolling down my neck, our shadows under the spotlight, and the rush of air from the helicopter as I said, "I love you."

About the Author

Azmi Abusam was born in Khartoum, Sudan, in 1990, attended Emory University, and published his first book, *The Night I Lost My Father's Gun*, in 2019. He lived in Oak Park, Illinois, and Columbia, South Carolina. After college, Azmi worked at National Public Radio, taught math and science in Washington, D.C., received a Master of Education degree from George Mason University, and joined his brother's tech startup as a product manager. His time is divided between family and friends, sports, music, and art.